The Joint Free Public Library
of
Morristown and Morris Township

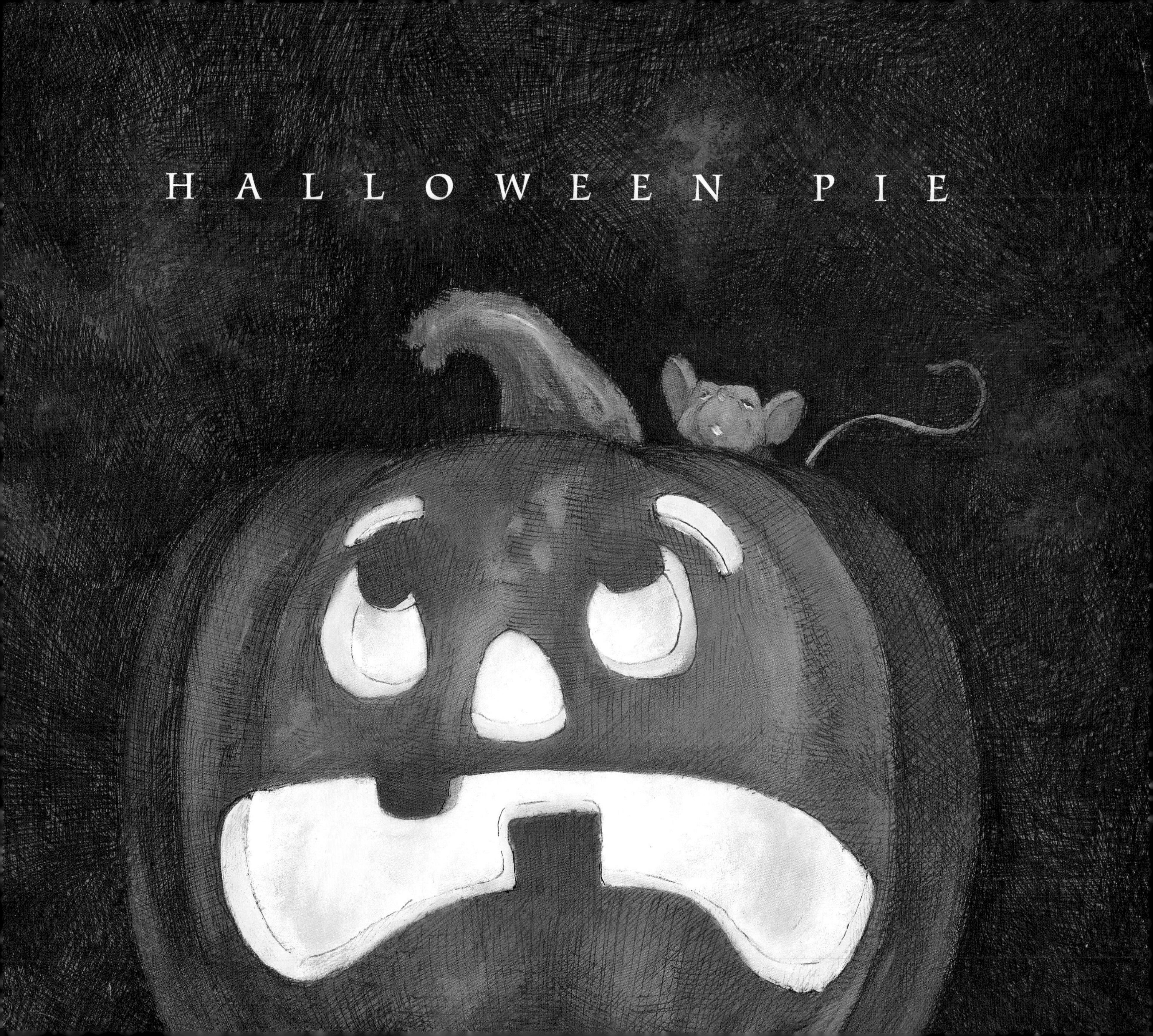
HALLOWEEN PIE

To Riley, our littlest spook
—MOT

To everyone who loves my favorite holiday, Halloween
—KO'M

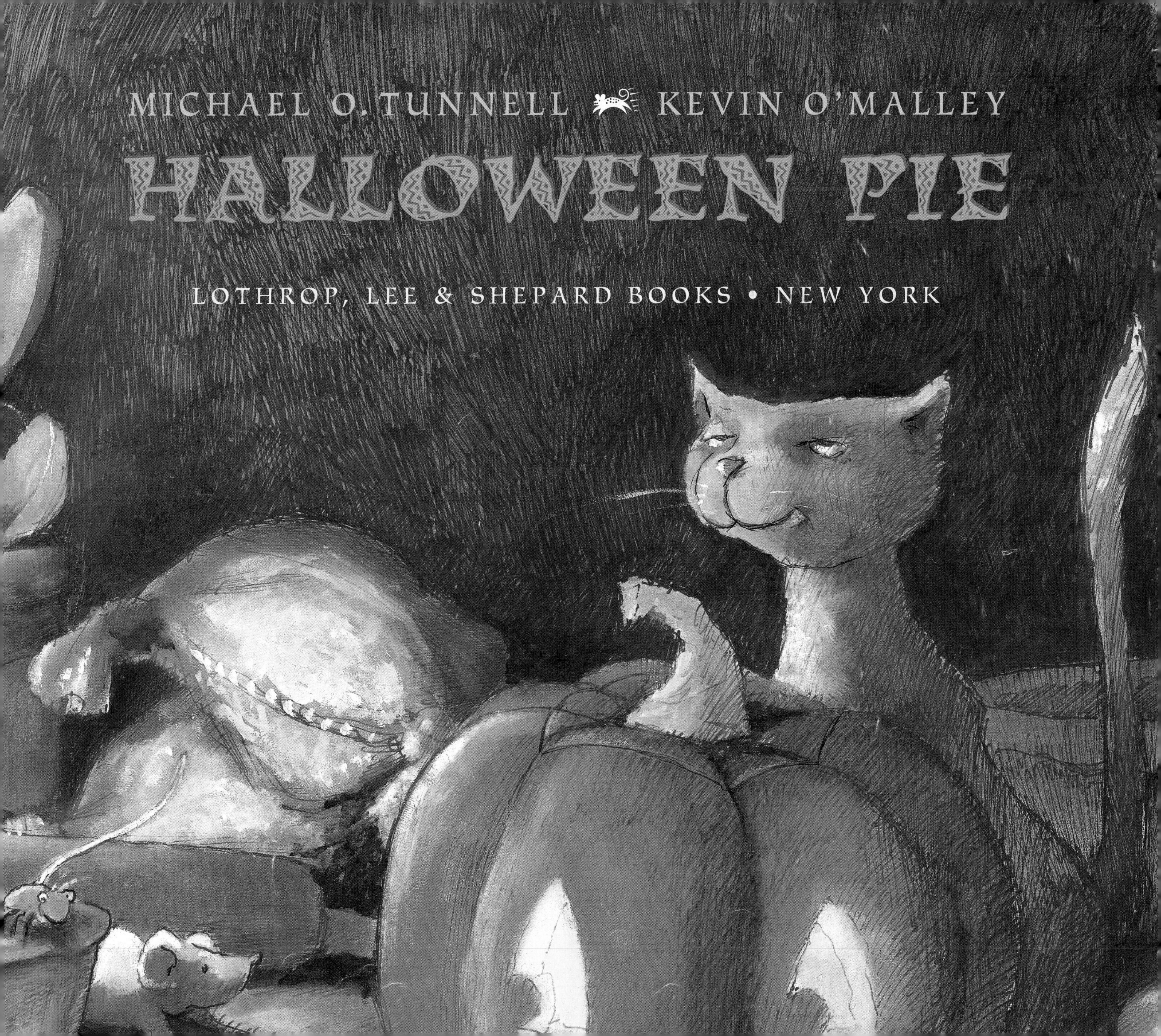

MICHAEL O. TUNNELL · KEVIN O'MALLEY

HALLOWEEN PIE

LOTHROP, LEE & SHEPARD BOOKS • NEW YORK

On Halloween, Old Witch baked a pie.
A pumpkin pie. A scrumptious pie.
A big-and-wide-as-a-full-moon pie.

Old Witch set the pie aside to cool. "Protect this treat," she mumbled, waving her arms and twitching her nose to make the spell complete. "Protect this treat . . . for me alone to eat."

Then she leaped on her broom and flew into the dark night to

Soon the wind began to blow. It blew down the chimney.
It blew out the window.

It blew through the trees and over the graveyard fence.
And with it went the spicy scent of Halloween pie....

Vampire in his box sniffed the wind.
Ghoul on his walk sniffed the wind.
Ghost on her cloud sniffed the wind.

Banshee in her shroud sniffed the wind.
Zombie in his cave sniffed the wind.
Skeleton in his grave sniffed the wind.

Then they all rose from the graveyard

and followed their noses to Old Witch's cottage.

"Give me some pie!" Vampire called.

"Give me some pie!" Ghoul bawled.

"Give me some pie!" Ghost sighed.

"Give me some pie!" Banshee cried.

"Give me some pie!" Zombie groaned.

"Give me some pie!" Skeleton moaned.

When no one answered, Vampire and Ghoul and Ghost decided to help themselves. Banshee and Zombie and Skeleton decided to help themselves too. Down the chimney, through the window, under the door they slipped. Then they ate and ate and ate until their tummies bulged. Their eyes grew heavy, and—just as the Halloween pie was gone—they began to yawn.

Vampire fell asleep before the fire. Ghoul tumbled into the bed.
Ghost dreamed in an empty drawer. Banshee snored high in the rafters.
Zombie dozed behind the door. Skeleton snoozed on the mantel.

And while they slumbered, the witch's spell began to work. Vampire grew round and firm as he snored. Ghoul fancied he heard the cluck-cluck of chickens. Ghost dreamed she was drowning in the salty sea. . . .

At midnight, Old Witch flew back to her cottage, where she found the door ajar. She peeked carefully through the window. She crept stealthily to the door. Then she sniffed and sniffed and sniffed—there was not a whiff of Halloween pie.

But Old Witch wasn't bothered a bit. She just smiled a crooked smile and stepped inside.

Loafing before the fire was a perfectly shaped pumpkin.
Buried in the bedding were a dozen brown eggs.
Scattered inside the drawer was a smidgen of salt.

Swinging from the rafters was a sack of sweet sugar.
Crouching behind the door was a crock of thick cream.
Sitting on the mantel were stacks of cinnamon sticks
and piles of spicy cloves and ginger.

All done!

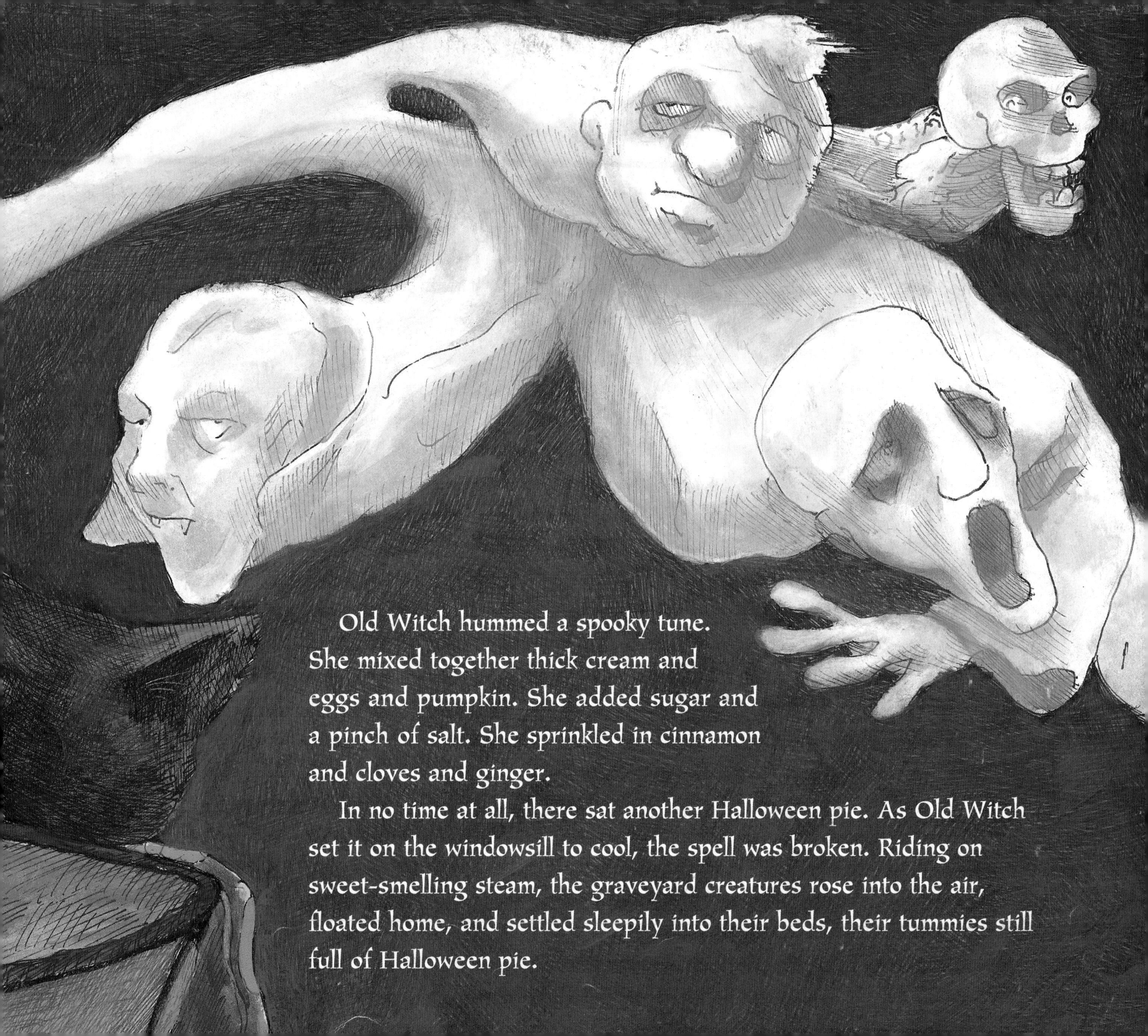

Old Witch hummed a spooky tune. She mixed together thick cream and eggs and pumpkin. She added sugar and a pinch of salt. She sprinkled in cinnamon and cloves and ginger.

In no time at all, there sat another Halloween pie. As Old Witch set it on the windowsill to cool, the spell was broken. Riding on sweet-smelling steam, the graveyard creatures rose into the air, floated home, and settled sleepily into their beds, their tummies still full of Halloween pie.

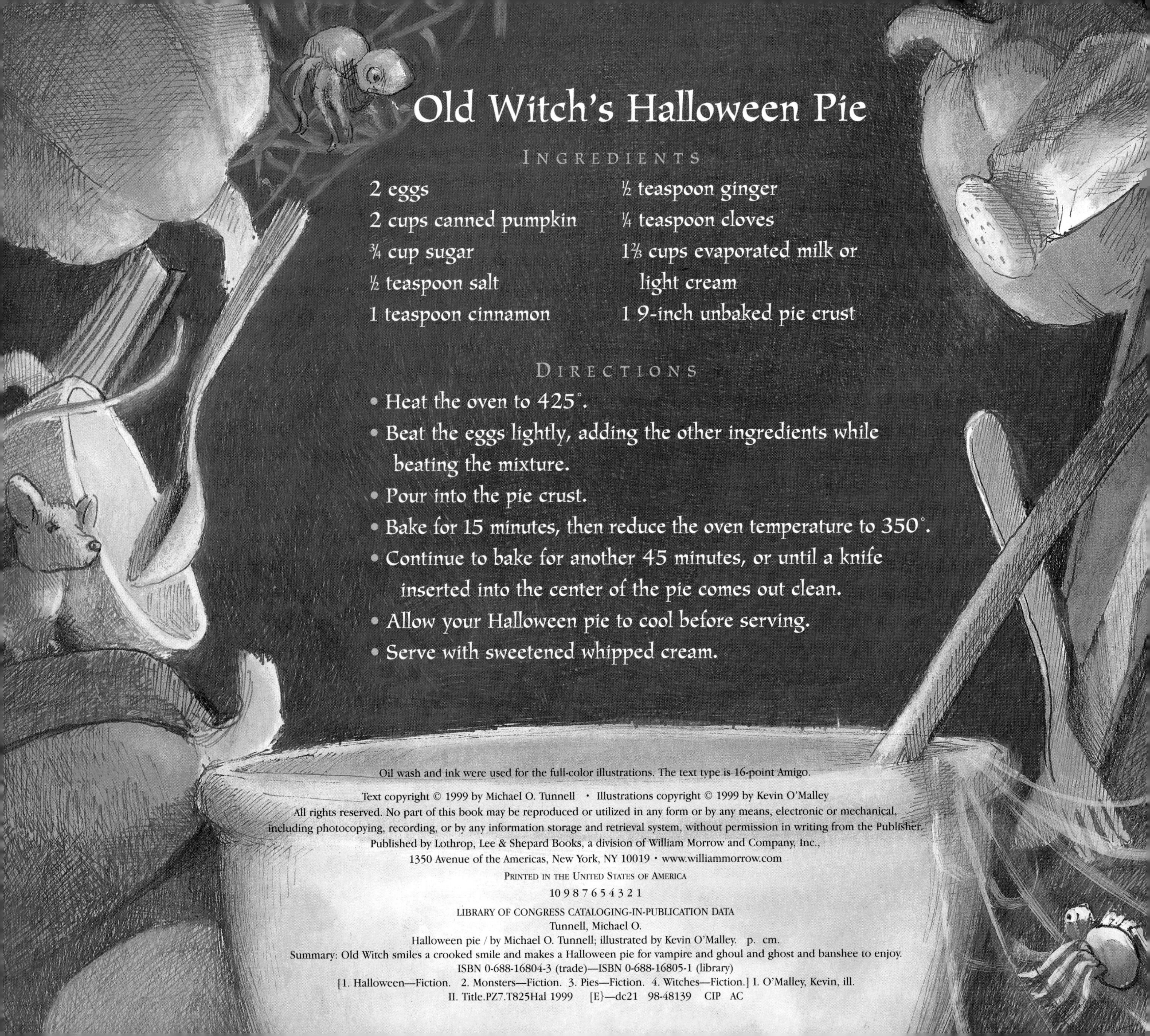

Old Witch's Halloween Pie

Ingredients

2 eggs
2 cups canned pumpkin
¾ cup sugar
½ teaspoon salt
1 teaspoon cinnamon
½ teaspoon ginger
¼ teaspoon cloves
1⅔ cups evaporated milk or light cream
1 9-inch unbaked pie crust

Directions

- Heat the oven to 425°.
- Beat the eggs lightly, adding the other ingredients while beating the mixture.
- Pour into the pie crust.
- Bake for 15 minutes, then reduce the oven temperature to 350°.
- Continue to bake for another 45 minutes, or until a knife inserted into the center of the pie comes out clean.
- Allow your Halloween pie to cool before serving.
- Serve with sweetened whipped cream.

Oil wash and ink were used for the full-color illustrations. The text type is 16-point Amigo.

Text copyright © 1999 by Michael O. Tunnell • Illustrations copyright © 1999 by Kevin O'Malley
All rights reserved. No part of this book may be reproduced or utilized in any form or by any means, electronic or mechanical, including photocopying, recording, or by any information storage and retrieval system, without permission in writing from the Publisher.

Published by Lothrop, Lee & Shepard Books, a division of William Morrow and Company, Inc.,
1350 Avenue of the Americas, New York, NY 10019 • www.williammorrow.com
Printed in the United States of America
10 9 8 7 6 5 4 3 2 1
LIBRARY OF CONGRESS CATALOGING-IN-PUBLICATION DATA
Tunnell, Michael O.
Halloween pie / by Michael O. Tunnell; illustrated by Kevin O'Malley. p. cm.
Summary: Old Witch smiles a crooked smile and makes a Halloween pie for vampire and ghoul and ghost and banshee to enjoy.
ISBN 0-688-16804-3 (trade)—ISBN 0-688-16805-1 (library)
[1. Halloween—Fiction. 2. Monsters—Fiction. 3. Pies—Fiction. 4. Witches—Fiction.] I. O'Malley, Kevin, ill.
II. Title.PZ7.T825Hal 1999 [E]—dc21 98-48139 CIP AC